Anansi's Party Time

Anansi's Party Time

by ERIC A. KIMMEL

illustrated by
JANET STEVENS

Holiday House / New York

To Janet

E. A. K

To Regina

J. S.

1 3 5 7 9 10 8 6 4 2
Library of Congress Cataloging-in-Publication Data
Kimmel, Eric A.
Anansi's party time / by Eric A. Kimmel ; illustrated by Janet Stevens. — 1st ed.
p. cm.
Summary: When Anansi the spider invites Turtle to a party just to play a trick on him, Turtle gets revenge at a party of his own.
ISBN 978-0-8234-1922-7 (hardcover)
1. Anansi (Legendary character)—Legends. [1. Anansi (Legendary character)—Legends. 2. Folklore—Africa, West.] I. Stevens, Janet, ill.
II. Title. PZ8.1.K567Apt 2008398.2—dc22   [E]   2007002206

Turtle and Anansi went fishing together.
Turtle played a trick on Anansi.
Anansi did not forget.
He waited a long time to get even.
Months later, long after Turtle had forgotten about the trick,
a letter from Anansi appeared in his mailbox.
The letter said . . .

Turtle moves very slowly.

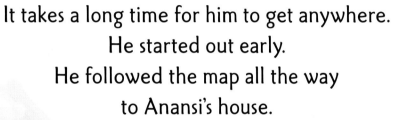

It takes a long time for him to get anywhere.
He started out early.
He followed the map all the way
to Anansi's house.

Knock, knock, knock! Turtle knocked on Anansi's door.

"I'm here!" Turtle said.

"What took you so long?" Anansi asked. "Where is your costume?"

"I didn't know it was a costume party," said Turtle.

"You know now. Go home and get a costume." Anansi slammed the door.

Turtle went home.

It took him a long time
to get there.

It took him a
long time . . .

to choose a costume.

It took him a long time to walk back to Anansi's house.

Knock, knock, knock! Turtle knocked on the door.

"Hippity-hop!" Turtle said when Anansi opened it. "Hippity-hop! Guess what I am!"

"You're a silly-looking turtle pretending to be a bunny," Anansi said. "Where's your dish?"

"What dish?" asked Turtle

"I told everyone to bring a dish," Anansi said.

"You didn't tell me," said Turtle.

"I just did. You need a dish. Go home and get one." Anansi slammed the door.

Turtle went home again.
It took him a long time.

It took him a long time to choose a dish.

He carried it back to
Anansi's house.

Knock, knock, knock! Turtle knocked on the door.

"I brought a dish. Can I come in?" Turtle asked Anansi.

Anansi looked at Turtle's dish. "Don't you know anything, Turtle? 'Bring a dish' means 'Bring something for everyone to eat.' Nobody can eat that plate. Go home and put something on it."

Turtle turned around and went home again.

He found his favorite recipe—chocolate turtles.

When the chocolate turtles cooled, he put them on the dish and carried them back to Anansi's house.

Knock, knock, knock! Turtle knocked on the door.

"Look, Anansi! I have a costume. I have a dish. I made chocolate turtles. Can I come to the party now?"

"The party's over. Everybody went home," Anansi said. "But thank you for the chocolate turtles. They look delicious. I'll eat them tomorrow."

Anansi slammed the door. Turtle heard him laughing on the other side. "Hee, hee, hee! Poor Turtle! What a doofus!"
"I've been tricked!" said Turtle.

A few days later a letter from Turtle appeared in Anansi's mailbox.

Dear Anansi,
   I'm having a party and you're
invited. Here is a map to my house.
   Don't wear a costume.
   Don't bring a dish.
   Be ready to have lots of fun.
   Don't be late!

                    Love,
                    Turtle

"Hooray! A party!" Anansi exclaimed. On the day of the party, he set out for Turtle's house. He followed the map to the river.

"Turtle's house is underwater. I will have to swim." Anansi took a deep breath and jumped into the river.

Sploosh!
He went to the bottom.

Fwoom!
He floated up to the top.

"I forgot that spiders float," said Anansi. "How can I get to Turtle's party if I can't get to the bottom of the river?"

Just then, he saw Crab walking by.

"Hello, Crab!" said Anansi. "Are you going to Turtle's party?"
"You bet!" Crab said. "Everybody's going!"
"Can I ride on your back?" asked Anansi.

"Get on. Hold tight
to my shell."
Anansi climbed onto
Crab's back. He held onto
the points of Crab's shell
with all eight legs.

Soon they arrived at Turtle's house. Turtle opened the door.
"Hello, Crab! Hello, Anansi! The party's just starting."
Everybody was having fun. Crab waved to his friends. Anansi didn't wave to anybody.
"I'm holding tight to Crab so I don't float," he explained.

"Would you like some punch?" asked Otter.

"Sure!" said Crab.

"Not for me!" said Anansi. "I'm holding on."

"How about cake and ice cream?" asked Hippo.

"Nope!" said Anansi. "I'm holding on."

"Can I have it?" asked Crab.

He ate two portions of cake and ice cream, his own and Anansi's.

"This party sure is fun," said Crab.

"Phooey!" said Anansi. This party wasn't fun for him. He couldn't drink punch. He couldn't eat cake or ice cream. He couldn't even wave to his friends. All he could do was hold on.

"Attention, everybody!" said Turtle. "Let's play Mystery Animal. I'm thinking of an animal who's here at the party. Whoever guesses who it is wins a prize."

"Oooh! Oooh! I'm great at games. I'm going to win," said Crab.

"Be quiet so I can hear the clues," Anansi said.

Turtle read the first clue. "Clue number one. The Mystery Animal is very small."

"Oooh!
Oooh! I know!" said
Crocodile. "It's me! I was
small when I was a baby."
"But you're not
small now," said Anansi.
"Next clue."

"Clue number two," said Turtle.

"The Mystery Animal is very clever."

"Oooh! Oooh! That's me!" yelled Hippo. "I'm clever."

"No way!" said Anansi. "You're not small either.

Are there any more clues?"

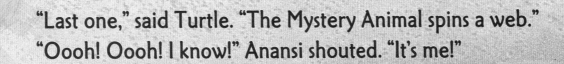

"Last one," said Turtle. "The Mystery Animal spins a web."
"Oooh! Oooh! I know!" Anansi shouted. "It's me!"

"That's right!" said Turtle. "Anansi wins the prize. Eight balloons!"
"Oh no!" yelled Anansi. "I don't want balloons. They'll make me float."